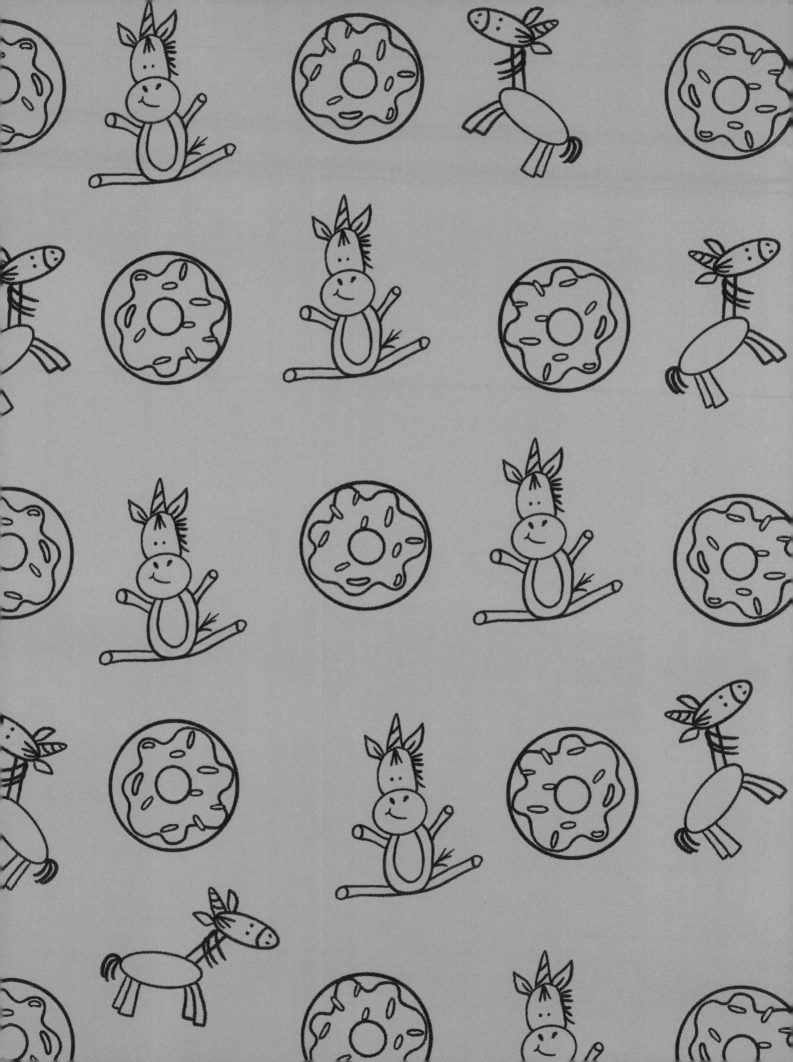

ACTUALLY MOMMY

An Along Came Abby Book

Written and Illustrated
By Lissa Terry

Published by Actually Mommy Books,
PO box 766, Westhampton Beach, NY 11978.

Actually Mommy by Lissa Terry
Illustrations by Lissa and Phoebe Terry
Summary: Abby interrupts her mom to showcase
her imaginative counting skills.

ISBN 9780578817460

For my two girls.

To my oldest daughter, Phoebe, whose amazing artistic abilities have their touch on every picture in this book, may you never stop creating.

To the youngest of the Terry clan, Abigail, who is the inspiration for every word in this book, may your imagination continue to grow with you!

Finally, to grandad Mike, you're no longer with us, but your amazing gift of storytelling lives in our hearts and our children.

-Lissa Terry

"There once was a family of seven, and then, along came Abby-"

"Actually, Mommy," said Abby, "my real name is Abigail, but most people call me **the Donut Defender**."

"There once was a little girl who loved unicorns-"

"Actually, Mommy," said Abby,

"today I am a unicorn,

and I have ten stuffed unicorns that I play with."

"There once was a little girl who
loved to wear a crown-"

"Actually, Mommy," said Abby,

"it's called a tiara,

and I have nine of them.

Sometimes I pretend they

are falling from the sky, and

I catch them."

"There once was a little girl who loved cookies to snack on-"

"Actually, Mommy," said Abby,

"the Cookie Fairy
and I like to eat
eight cookies
for breakfast.

But only on special days."

"There once was a little girl who loved to jump in the pool-"

"Actually, Mommy," said Abby,

"I do cannon balls.

I can do seven in a row, without my swimmies."

"There once was a little girl
who loved donuts,
but so did her brothers."

"Actually, Mommy," said Abby,

"there are six
donuts in the
kitchen right now!

But don't worry about those boys,

I'm in charge of the eye-ing!"

"There once was a little girl whose big sister was an artist-"

"Actually, Mommy," said Abby,

"I am an artist, too.
And I've painted you five beautiful paintings:
three donuts and two potato people."

"There once was a little girl who didn't like broccoli-"

"Actually, Mommy, it's ok because I like carrots.

If I eat four, can I have a chocolate egg?"

"There once was a little girl
who loved tigers-"

"Actually, Mommy," said Abby,

"I am a baby tiger.

But I can roar as loud as

three tigers...

ROAR!!!"

"There once was a little girl who loved her daddy-"

"Actually, Mommy," said Abby,

"Daddy's real name is Wonder Boop!

And Wonder Boop and Donut Defender are the two greatest superheroes."

"Actually, Abby," said Mommy,
"being a superhero is great,

but I love the little things you do:

how you encourage your friends
with kind words, how you hug
your sister when no one else
sees she's sad,

"and how you make brownies for your brothers when they never leave any for you."

"Actually, Mommy," said Abby,

"I put magic jumping beans in my brothers' brownies!!"

"There once was one little girl whose mind was full of beautiful adventures and stories.

She was noble and charitable.

"She loved to make people smile and knew the importance of kindness and being a good friend."

"Actually, Mommy," said Abby,

"I think that girl is me!"

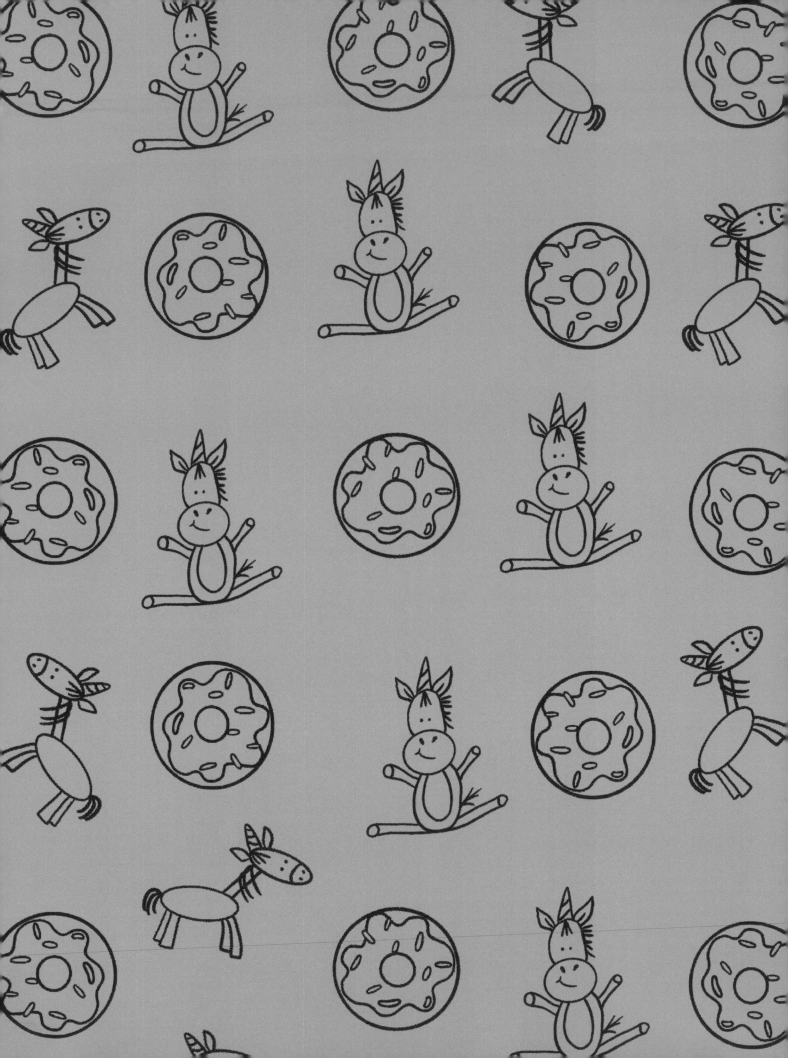

CPSIA information can be obtained
at www.ICGtesting.com
Printed in the USA
BVHW051216020421
603979BV00002B/2